MOST DAYS

For Mom, who taught me to notice
the little things I love so much.
—M.L.

For Mom and Dad.
—M.E.B.

MOST DAYS

WORDS BY
MICHAEL LEANNAH

PICTURES BY
MEGAN ELIZABETH BARATTA

TILBURY HOUSE PUBLISHERS, THOMASTON, MAINE

Most days are ordinary days. I get out of bed.
I walk to the bathroom. I brush my teeth.

I get dressed. I look at the person looking back at me from the mirror. I'm one day older than yesterday.

I look into the eyes of the goldfish. She looks into mine. She is one day older, too.

A splash of sunlight plays on the kitchen floor. Voices murmur. I smell toast, hear a spoon in a cereal bowl. It's a plain old ordinary day.

But wait! The plant on the windowsill had six leaves yesterday, and today there are seven.

Outside, bees drone. A dog barks. A car door shuts. Everything is the same.

Or is it? That spiderweb wasn't there yesterday, and the puddle I splashed in is gone.

A pine tree whispers to me. Today is new, it says.

Things don't happen the same way twice—
that blue jay talking to us, that friend
calling hello. The wind has blown yesterday's
air far away, and the air we're breathing
now will be miles from here tomorrow.

A cat on a window seat watches the neighborhood. A cloud drags its shadow down the street.

The world puts on a
show, as it does every day.

A man plays a saxophone on a porch.
The bakery on the corner fills the air with the aroma of fresh bread.
Trucks rumble. Bulldozers roar.

If this were winter, there would be frost on windows.

If it were spring, I could see dew on new grass.

If it were autumn,
leaves would
rustle underfoot.

But on this summer day, sunlight
sparkles on the river like diamonds.
What a wonderful plain old ordinary day!

The world is moving, and I am too. Sometimes when the day is busy and the minutes go by too fast, I forget to notice the little things I love so much: the sweet smell of grass in the wind, the wagging of my dog's tail.

Good things happen in the
ordinary minutes of an ordinary day.

A hug.
Laughter.
Dinner cooking.

A soft breeze drifts in through an open window. I snuggle next to someone I love as she turns the pages of a book. The dog snores. A clock ticks. A sliver of moon hangs in the sky.

When I go to bed, this day's ordinary minutes glimmer
in my memory like stars in the night sky. Another day
will come tomorrow, full of extraordinary things filling
ordinary minutes. An ordinary day, a good day . . .

. . . like most days.

Michael Leannah was a teacher in elementary schools for more than 30 years and is the author of an instruction manual for teachers, *We Think with Ink*, and the picture book *Most People*. His children's fiction has been published in *Highlights for Children, Ladybug*, and other magazines. A resident of Wisconsin, he is a father and proud grandfather.

Megan Elizabeth Baratta illustrates with a blend of pencil, watercolor, and digital media. *Most Days* is her debut children's book. She loves rendering scenes of ordinary life and showing their quiet beauty. Megan lives in upstate New York with her husband, Jeremy, where she enjoys cooking, reading, and sipping coffee.

Tilbury House Publishers • www.tilburyhouse.com

Text © 2021 by Michael Leannah • Illustrations © 2021 by Megan Elizabeth Baratta

15 16 17 18 19 20 XXX 10 9 8 7 6 5 4 3 2 1

Library of Congress Control Number: 2020945400

Designed by Frame25 Productions • Printed in China